5x
FRAGILE
BANANAS
COFFEE
HEAVY

Boxitects

REFRIGERATOR
HANDLE WITH CARE

Boxitects

by Kim Smith

CLARION BOOKS
Houghton Mifflin Harcourt | Boston New York

MEG was a boxitect.
She loved to make things out of boxes.

CUTLERY
FRAGILE

She loved making
tiny houses,

tall towers,

and twisty tunnels.

And she made marvelous things
no one had ever seen before!

Meg was proud of her work.
She could make boxes into anything.
Meg's mother was proud too.
She thought Meg was brilliant and creative.

So Meg's mother sent Meg to Maker School
where she could be even more brilliant and creative.

At Maker School there were blanketeers, spaghetti-tects, tin-foilers, and egg-cartoneers. There was almost any kind of maker you could imagine!

But Meg was the class's first boxitect, and that made her feel special.

At school, Meg learned all about boxitecture.

She learned how to make her structures useful,

strong,

and beautiful.

Meg loved everything about maker school . . .

. . . until Simone showed up.

Like Meg, Simone was new.
She was also brilliant and creative.
Worst of all, Simone was a boxitect too.

And she was already making things
Meg had never dreamed of.

In class, Simone would point out ways
Meg could make her constructions
a little straighter,

more wind resistant,

and less boring.

So Meg told Simone she should build things that were less bumpy,

sturdier,

and much prettier.

On the last day of school, the class's annual Maker Match was held to see who could make the MOST amazing thing.

There was just one rule: You had to work as a team. But Meg didn't want to work with anyone. And neither did Simone.

The blanketeers built with blankets and pillows.

The spaghetti-tects built with pasta and glue.

The bake-ologists built with cake and frosting.

But the boxitects were not building at all.

They were arguing.
"I want to make a treehouse!" Meg said.
"No, I want to make a ship!" Simone insisted.

Meg drew a line down the middle of a very large box.
"I'll take this half. You can have the other."
"Fine!" said Simone.

Soon Meg noticed that her treehouse wasn't as large as Simone's ship. So she made her side taller and more impressive.

When Simone noticed that Meg's treehouse was taller than her ship, she made *her* side higher and more extraordinary.

Slowly, Meg and Simone's creation grew bigger and bigger.

They both built and built until there wasn't a single box left.

And at last . . .

FRAG

. . . they finished.

"What is it?" asked a classmate.

"I've never seen anything like it," said another.

The teacher said, "It looks like it might . . ."

FRAGILE
ACHOO!

CR

ASH!
HEAVY

"Your side was too wobbly!" shouted Meg.
"Your side was too heavy!" cried Simone.
"Oh dear," said the judge.

The Maker Match was not over yet,
but most of Meg and Simone's work was ruined.

There were only a few parts left
that could be saved.

"If we combine my treehouse with your ship . . ." Meg started.
". . . we might be able to make one thing," finished Simone.

The boxitects decided to call a truce
so they could finish the match.

Working as a team, Meg and Simone quickly joined the remaining pieces together until . . .

. . . they had created something new.

At the end of the Maker Match,
the boxitects hadn't won first place.

But they had a different way of
making brilliant and creative things—
working together.

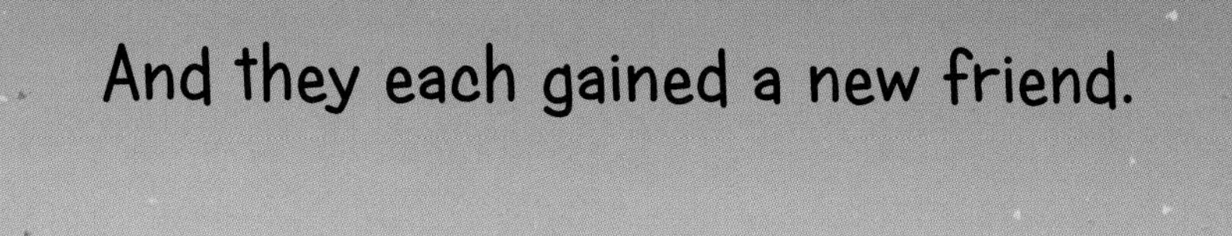
And they each gained a new friend.

What should we make next?
How about a buoyant bungalow?
Or a motorcycle mansion?

Why is cardboard so extraordinary?

An experiment!

Cardboard boxes are so amazing because they're corrugated! Corrugated means there is a piece of folded material sandwiched between two flat pieces of the same material. This makes cardboard super strong and super light. Let's try making our own corrugated cardboard.

Supplies

- 2 pieces of paper that are the same size
- 1 longer piece of paper
- a small object such as a toy

First, stack the 3 pieces of paper and try to balance your object on top.

Did it fall off?

Now let's try balancing the object again on corrugated paper!

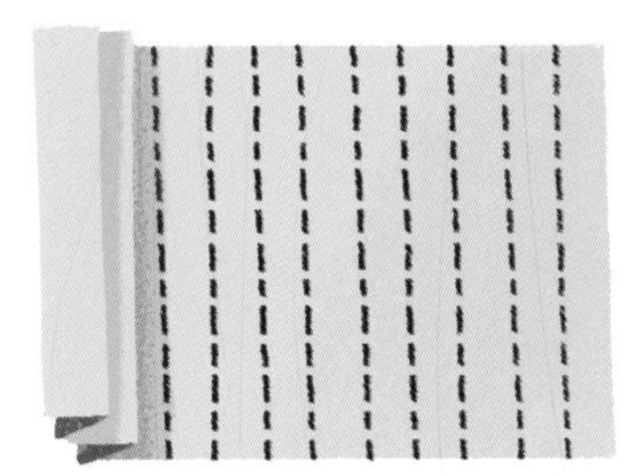

Fold the long piece of paper like a fan.

Expand the folded piece and place it in between the two flat sheets.

Now try balancing the object again!

Boxitect Challenge: What can make your cardboard even stronger? Try different sizes of fans, or different kinds of paper to see what holds up best.

Be a Boxitect!

How does Meg turn completely ordinary boxes into extraordinary things? All it takes is imagination! Here are two projects to get you started on your way to designing and building your own creations.

Supplies

- At least 3 large cardboard boxes. The more boxes you have, the longer your tunnel will be.
- Duct tape
- Craft knife and/or scissors (Ask an adult for help with the cutting!)
- Paint, markers, stickers, etc.

Build a Boxitect Tunnel:

1. Open up both ends of each box.

2. Line up boxes in a row with flaps slightly overlapping.

3. Tape the boxes together with duct tape.

4. Cut out any windows and doors you want.

5. Decorate your new tunnel!

Boxitect Challenge: Make your tunnel unique! Try a door made of streamers, using a string of lights, or even adding a cardboard periscope! If you have a lot of boxes, try making a tunnel maze!

Supplies

- 1 large cardboard box
- 4 medium boxes (roughly similar in size)
- Duct tape
- Scissors or craft knife (Be sure to have an adult help with the cutting!)
- Paint, markers, stickers, etc.
- String or yarn

Build a Boxitect Castle:

1. Open flaps of 2 medium boxes and tape the boxes together to form a column. Do the same with the other 2 medium boxes.

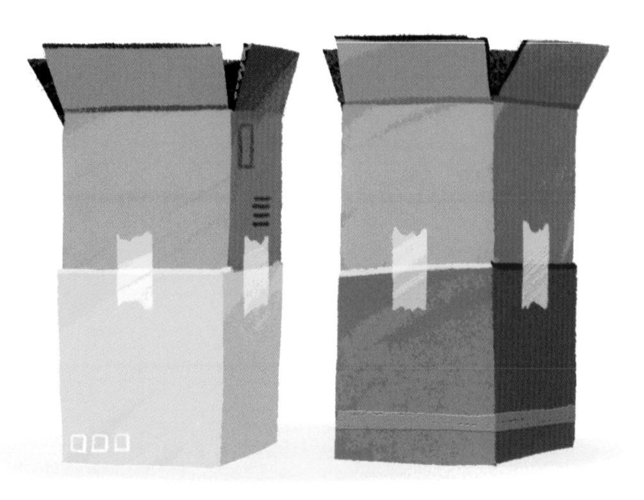

2. Tape the flaps at the top of the 2 columns and the flaps of the large box so the top flaps are standing up.

3. Cut the tops of the large box and columns into a crown pattern.

4. Draw an upside down U-shape door on the front of the large box and cut along the line, leaving the bottom of the door attached, and fold the door downward.

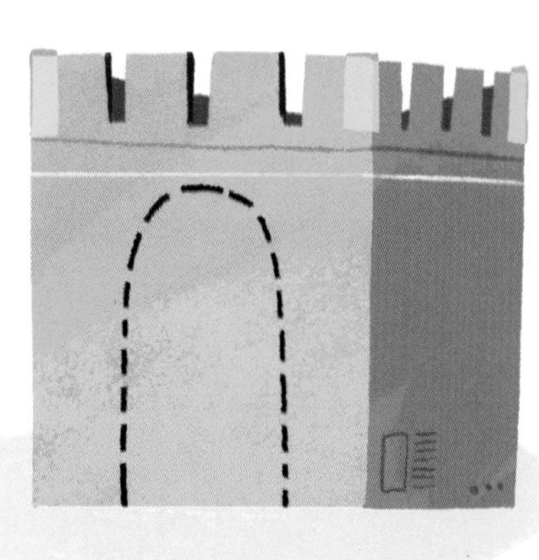

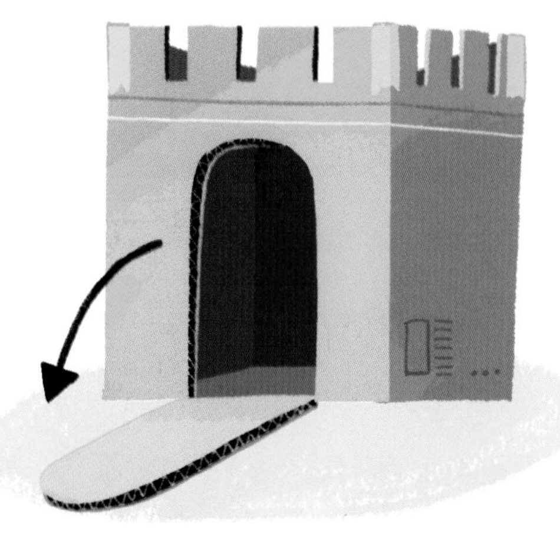

5. At the top of the door, punch a small hole in either side and in either side of the doorway. Run a string through the hole in one side of the door and through the hole in the same side of the large box. Tie knots in both ends of the string to secure. Repeat on the other side of the doorway.

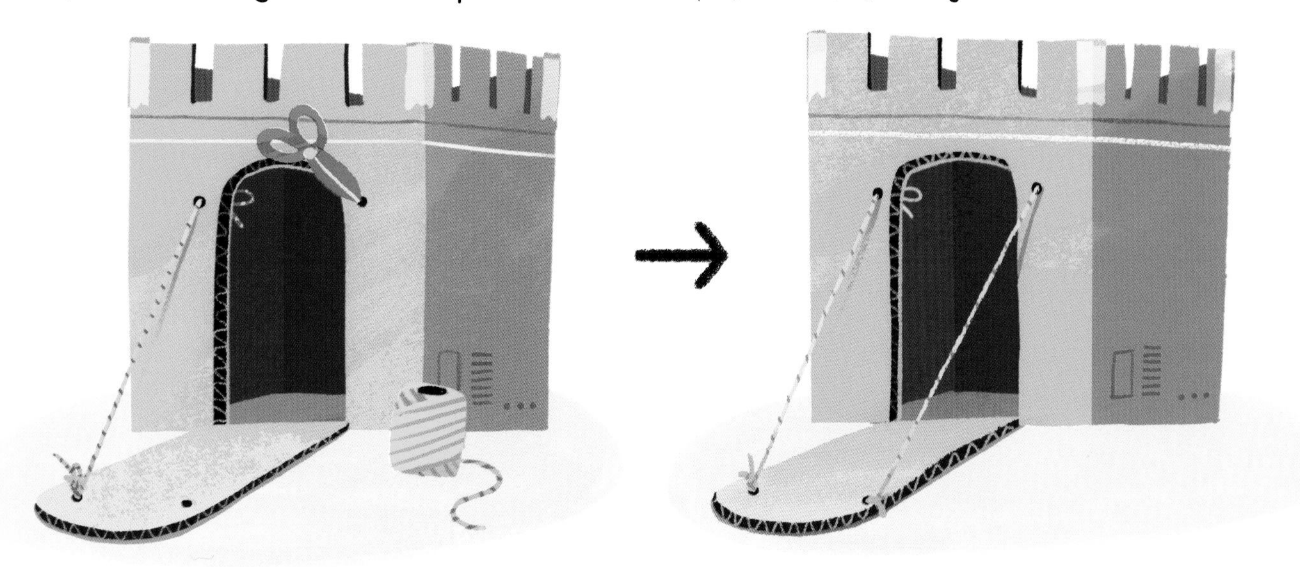

6. Draw two windows on the top of the columns and cut out.

7. Tape columns to large box, if desired, and decorate your castle!

Boxitect Challenge: Castles have many different passageways and rooms including, sometimes, secret ones! Can you find a way to connect the towers inside the main part of the castle? Can you add more towers or walls to make your castle bigger?

To all makers, constructors, creators, and inventors.

And a special thanks to the wonderful book-itects
who made this possible: Kelly, Jennifer, Sharismar, and Suzanne.

CLARION BOOKS | 3 Park Avenue, New York, New York 10016 | | Clarion Books is an imprint of Houghton Mifflin Harcourt Publishing Company. | hmhbooks.com
The illustrations in this book were created digitally in Photoshop. | The text was set in Candy Round BTN. | Book design by Sharismar Rodriguez
Library of Congress Cataloging-in-Publication Data | Names: Smith, Kim, 1986– author, illustrator. | Title: Boxitects / Kim Smith. | Description: Boston; New York : Clarion Books, Houghton Mifflin Harcourt, [2020] | Summary: Meg goes to Maker School to hone her talent for building with boxes, but when Simone, another boxitect, arrives they become so competitive they nearly fail in the annual Maker Match. | Identifiers: LCCN 2018051997
ISBN 9781328477200 (hardcover picture book) | Subjects: | CYAC: Boxes—Fiction. | Architecture—Fiction. | Competition (Psychology)—Fiction.
Classification: LCC PZ7.1.S64 Box 2020 | DDC [E]—dc23 | LC record available at https://lccn.loc.gov/2018051997
Manufactured in USA | PHX 4500823294

HEAVY
KITCH
4
BATH
PAPER
FRAGILE